ISBN 978-0-553-52114-6
randomhousekids.com
Printed in the United States of America
10 9 8 7 6 5 4 3 2 1

Random House Children's Books supports the First Amendment and celebrates the right to read.

BUBBLE GUPPIES

MEET BUBBLE KITTY!

Adapted by **Mary Man-Kong**

Based on the teleplay "Bubble Kitty!" by Melinda LaRose,
with additional writing by Jonny Belt, Lucas Mills, and Robert Scull

Illustrated by **Eren Unten**

 A GOLDEN BOOK • NEW YORK

Gil and Molly were swimming to school when they heard a faint noise.

"*Meow!*"

"Hey! Look!" Gil exclaimed. "A little cat!"

"She's so cute!" said Molly. "I think she likes Bubble Puppy."

Gil and Molly played with the kitty, but soon they had to leave for school. The little kitty wanted to go with them.

"Sorry, kitty-cat, but you should stay here,"
Gil said. "Somebody might be looking for you."

At school, Gil and Molly told Mr. Grouper
and their friends about the little kitty.
Just then, they heard a meowing sound.
"It's coming from outside," Goby said.

They all rushed to the door—and there was
the kitty! She had followed Molly and Gil to school.

Mr. Grouper picked up the kitten and looked at her collar. "It says her name is Bubble Kitty."

"Well, that's convenient," said Deema with a laugh.

Mr. Grouper told the Guppies that Bubble Kitty was related to big cats in the wild.

"Little cats and big cats have a lot in common," said Mr. Grouper. "Cats can see in the dark with their special eyes. And all cats have a long, furry . . ."

"Tail!" Nonny finished.

Mr. Grouper nodded. "Cats use their tails to help them balance. And cats walk quietly on their . . ."

"Paws!" Goby said.

On the other side of the classroom, Deema was playing store. Gil asked Deema if there was a spot where his black leopard could play.

"You've come to the *purr*-fect place!" Deema said. "We can build him a jungle gym!"

After they finished making the jungle gym, Gil placed his black leopard inside. It gave a happy roar.

"Another *cat*-isfied customer," Deema said, laughing.

Next, Gil wanted to pretend to be a big-game photographer. "That means I take pictures of big cats," Gil told Molly. "Do you see? There's a tiger in the bushes."

Molly and Gil quietly waited for the tiger to appear.

Suddenly, Bubble Puppy jumped up behind Gil.
"Arf! Arf! Arf!" barked the puppy.
"Ahhh!" Gil cried.

In the classroom, the Bubble Guppies
pretended to be different big cats.
"I'm a leopard," said Deema.
"I like to sleep in the treetops."
"I'm a lion," said Nonny. *"Roar!"*

"I'm a cheetah. Cheetahs are the fastest cats in the world," Gil said, zipping past his friends. Everyone laughed—except Bubble Kitty.

"What's the matter, Bubble Kitty?" asked
Oona. "Don't you want to play?"
Bubble Kitty meowed sadly.
"I think Bubble Kitty misses her home," Oona
said. "Maybe we can help find her owner."

"That's a great idea!" exclaimed Mr. Grouper. The Guppies used a picture of Bubble Kitty to make a flyer. Then Mr. Grouper added his telephone number. He promised to make copies and put them up all over town.

When they went outside for playtime, the Bubble Guppies pretended to be on an African big-cat reserve.

"A reserve is a safe place for animals to live," said Nonny.

"Three baby cats are lost," reported Gil.
"Cat herders, we must find them! But watch
out for the Cat Burglar!"

First, the Bubble Guppies looked in the high
grasses of Africa. They saw a small, tawny cat.

"A baby lion!" exclaimed Goby.

"Babies of big cats are called cubs," said Nonny.

As Oona put the cute lion cub in her scooter's sidecar, suddenly she saw the Cat Burglar! "Here, kitty, kitty, kitty!" called the Cat Burglar.

Oona and her friends jumped on their
scooters and scooted out of there fast!
"We need to find a tiger cub," said Goby.
"Tiger cubs live in India. Let's try to find
the tiger cub before the Cat Burglar does!"

The friends imagined they had traveled all the way to India.

"Hmmm," said Goby. "I wonder where we should look for the tiger cub."

"Tigers like to swim," Oona said, pointing to a pool of water. "Look! There's the tiger cub!"

Oona put the tiger cub in Goby's sidecar, but then she saw the Cat Burglar again.

"Here, kitty, kitty, kitty!" called the Cat Burglar.

"Cat Burglar!" yelled Oona and Goby as they jumped on their scooters and zoomed off.

Next, the cat herders drove to Peru to look for a jaguar cub.

"Jaguars like to climb," said Oona. "Should we look for the jaguar cub by the lake, in the meadow, or in the jungle?"

lake

meadow

jungle

"The jungle!" exclaimed Goby. "There are lots of trees for a jaguar to climb in the jungle."

Soon Oona found a jaguar cub in a tree. She was about to take the cub back to her scooter, when the Cat Burglar blocked her path!

"Meow!" said the little lion cub, trying to protect his friends.

"Well, isn't that cute," the Cat Burglar said, laughing as he reached for the lion cub.

"Roar!" said the lion cub's dad, jumping out of the bushes. The lion roared so loudly that it frightened the Cat Burglar.

"I just wanted to pet the kitties," the Cat Burglar cried.

The Bubble Guppies felt bad for the Cat Burglar, so they decided to give him a new job.

"Your job is to keep the cats safe in the reserve," said Oona.

"Woo! I'm a cat herder!" exclaimed the Cat Burglar.

The Bubble Guppies cheered.

When playtime was over, the guppies returned to their classroom.

"Come quick!" Oona called. "Bubble Kitty's owner saw the flyer and called Mr. Grouper. We're going to take her home!"

"Field trip!" the Bubble Guppies exclaimed.

Mr. Grouper and the Bubble Guppies
piled into a safari jeep and drove toward
the mountains.
"Here we are!" said Mr. Grouper.
"This is where Bubble Kitty's owner lives."

"Yoo-hoo!" called a voice. "I'm up here!"

It was Ranger Katie. She was on the mountain making a large leopard sculpture.

"I'll be right down— Whoooaahhh!"
Ranger Katie had slipped and was dangling
from the sculpture!
"Meow!" cried Bubble Kitty. She jumped
out of the jeep and ran up the path.
"Follow that cat!" exclaimed Mr. Grouper.

"Hang on!" Mr. Grouper called to Ranger Katie
when they reached the top of the mountain.
"We need something to pull her up with,"
said Molly.

"What about this?" asked Deema. She handed
Molly the end of a big ball of yarn.

"Grab on!" Mr. Grouper shouted, quickly tossing one end of the yarn over the edge of the mountain. "Got it!" Ranger Katie called.

"Come on, everyone, pull!" shouted Mr. Grouper. They all formed a line and pulled and pulled. But it was no use—they couldn't pull the ranger up.

"We need more help!" cried Deema.

Bubble Puppy swam to the end of the line and pulled hard on the rope.

"Bubble Puppy's helping!" exclaimed Gil.

With Bubble Puppy and Bubble Kitty, the Bubble Guppies were able to pull Ranger Katie to safety!

"Thank you all for bringing my little kitty
back home," said the ranger. "And thank you
for saving me, too!"

"Meow!" Bubble Kitty purred her thanks
to Bubble Puppy before licking his face.

"Awww!" said the Bubble Guppies.

"What were you doing up there?" Gil asked Ranger Katie.

"I was working on this," said the ranger. "Presenting some of the greatest cats in the world: the leopard, the lion, the tiger . . ."

". . . and my favorite cat of all."

"It's Bubble Kitty!" exclaimed Molly.

"Ladies and gentlemen, *Meownt* Rushmore!" declared Ranger Katie.

"Whoo-hoo!" cheered the Bubble Guppies.